Stella Batts

None of Your Beeswax

Book

7

Courtney Sheinmel

Illustrated by Jennifer A. Bell

For my dad

—Courtney

For Roger

—Jennifer

Text Copyright © 2014 Courtney Sheinmel
Illustrations Copyright © 2014 Jennifer A. Bell

Sleeping Bear Press™

315 East Eisenhower Parkway, Suite 200 • Ann Arbor, MI 48108 • www.sleepingbearpress.com
© Sleeping Bear Press

M&Ms® and Skittles® are registered trademarks of Mars, Incorporated. Red Hots® is a registered trademark of the Ferrara Pan Candy Company. Oreo® is a registered trademark of Kraft Foods. Pop Rocks® is a registered trademark of Zeta Espacial S.A.

Printed and bound in the United States.
10 9 8 7 6 5 4 3 2 1

Library of Congress Cataloging-in-Publication Data • Sheinmel, Courtney. • Stella Batts : none of your beeswax / written by Courtney Sheinmel ; illustrated by Jennifer A. Bell. • pages cm. — (Stella Batts ; book 7) • Summary: "Eight-year-old Stella finds it is not easy or fun to keep secrets. The first secret is keeping her sister, Penny, from discovering that her pet fish has died and been replaced with a new fish. The second secret involves a school assignment which Stella cannot share even with her best friend"—Provided by the publisher. • ISBN 978-1-58536-853-2 (hard cover) — ISBN 978-1-58536-854-9 (paperback) • [1. Secrets—Fiction. 2. Family life—Fiction. 3. Schools—Fiction.] I. • Bell, Jennifer A., illustrator. II. Title. III. Title: None of your beeswax. • PZ7. S54124Stg 2014 • [Fic]—dc23 • 2014005114

Table of Contents

Introduction 7

Come Quick! 11

Can You Keep a Secret? 27

Close Calls 39

Current Events 59

None of Your Beeswax 73

Some Things Are Too Personal 83

Dad's Secret 97

Thursday 121

Everyone Finds Out 137

Stella Jr. 159

Introduction

Hi, I'm Stella Batts and here is a list of seven things about me:

 My name is Stella. (Oops, you knew that already.)

 I'm eight years old.

3. I live in Somers, California, with my mom, my dad, my sister, Penny, and my baby brother, Marco.

4. My family owns a candy store called Batts Confections—we named it that because Batts is our last name and confections is a fancy word for candy.

5. Of all the things they sell at Batts Confections, fudge is my very favorite.

6. Some of my other favorite things are dolphins, the TV show *Superstar Sam*, and the color purple, since that was the color of my dress at Aunt Laura's wedding.

7. Okay this is number seven—did you know that this is my SEVENTH book, and did you know seven is a lucky number? I don't know why. But it doesn't matter, because it's time to get on with the story.

Usually when Marco's in his swing, he doesn't cry at all. Unless he gets hungry, or if he needs a diaper change. So Dad could do things like read the newspaper, and I could do things like . . . well, right then I was a little bit bored, just waiting for Lucy to show up.

"Dad, I'm bored," I said.

CHAPTER 1

Come Quick!

Mom and Penny were sitting at the kitchen table, even though it wasn't time for any meal. It was an hour past breakfast, but still way before lunch. They were bent over a piece of paper, and Mom was pointing to something it said.

I came up behind them. "Strawberries, string cheese, orange juice," I read out loud.

"Stella-uh-uh!" Penny cried. My name is supposed to be two syllables, but Penny had turned it into four. "You were supposed to let me read!"

"But you don't know how to read," I said.

"I do, too," she said. "I know a lot of reading for someone who's only five. Tell her, Mom!"

"She's working on it," Mom said. "If you keep practicing, you'll be a great reader!"

"See," Penny said.

"Try the next word on our grocery list," Mom told her. She tapped the paper with her finger, and then raised it to her mouth to give me the *Shhh* sign.

"K . . . ka . . . kal," Penny said. "I don't know. That one's too hard."

"Kale," I read out loud. "Hmm, I think maybe Mom wrote that one down wrong. I've never heard of that food before in my whole entire life."

"Kale is a green veggie," Mom said.

"A green veggie?" I asked. "Like aspa and broccoli?"

"Oh, yum!" Penny exclaimed, at the s time that I said, "Oh, yuck!"

"Come on, Pen," Mom said. "Let's going."

Penny grabbed her favorite stuffe animal, a duck-billed platypus named Belinda "Belinda wants to see what kale looks like," she explained. She and Mom—and Belinda—left. I didn't have to go with them because Lucy was coming over. But she wasn't there yet, so it was just Dad and me and Baby Marco at home. Dad was sitting on the couch in the living room, reading the *California Gazette*. Marco was in his little baby swing, which is right next to the couch. You wind it up, and it swings back and forth, back and forth.

Dad lowered the paper and looked over at me. "Why don't you write in your book?"

"I finished my book," I told him. "And nothing new has happened so far for me to write about in my next one. Can we play a game?"

"Such as?"

"Such as . . ." I paused to think. "Ooh! I've got it! You can tell me that Batts Confections secret!"

The top floor of our candy store is under construction, but Dad won't tell Penny or me what he's building.

"That's not really a game, is it?" Dad said. "And it would ruin the surprise."

"I don't really like surprises," I reminded him. "I like to know what's going on—then I can know whether or not it's good."

"You've got to trust me on this," Dad said.

"Here, why don't we read the paper together?"

He handed me a section of the newspaper. I flipped it open and started to read. It didn't have good stories in it, just boring ones. I flipped the page again. "My fingers are turning black!" I said.

"It's from the ink on the page," Dad told me.

I wiped my hands on my jeans. "This paper is boring, and a little bit gross."

"Mmm hmm," Dad said, not really listening.

I glanced over at Marco. He was swinging back and forth, back and forth, and I stuck my tongue out at him. Not to be mean, just because that's his new trick. If you stick your tongue out, he sticks his tongue out, too. Mom calls it, "Monkey see, monkey do."

Marco stuck his tongue out.

Ring! Ring! went the doorbell. "I bet that's Lucy!" I shouted.

I opened the door and pulled Lucy inside. "You're finally here. Now the fun can begin."

"What kind of fun?" she asked.

"All kinds of kinds," I told her.

But first Lucy took off her shoes. That's what you have to do when you come to our house. Mom says shoes bring in too many germs, since you walk around in the dirty outside world all day long. She's been extra strict about it since Marco was born.

Speaking of Marco, the first thing Lucy said was, "Can I see the baby?"

Everyone always wants to see the baby. "Sure," I told her.

But when we got to the living room, Marco had fallen asleep, so all we could do was look at him. Being a baby is sort of like being a painting in a museum. People come in and want to look at you. But after that, there's not much else to do.

"We're going to go to my room while Marco sleeps and you read the boring paper,"

I told Dad.

"Lucy, I have a question for you," Dad said. "Stella thinks the newspaper is boring, but I think it's a fascinating window of what's going on in the world. Just look at this." He held out the section of the paper I'd left on the coffee table. "Esther Smyth, founder of the Somers Playhouse, lived to be a hundred years old."

"Did she die?" Lucy asked.

Dad nodded. "But this article is all about the amazing things she did with her life, all right here in Somers. Right where you're growing up—she walked these same streets a hundred years ago. That's pretty interesting, don't you think?"

I shrugged my shoulders. Lucy shrugged hers, too.

"Now they're changing the name of the

Playhouse on Camden Avenue to the Esther Smyth Arts Center, in her honor," Dad said. "And that's the kind of thing you learn about when you read the paper—that's why I love reading it every morning. I loved writing for it, too."

"When did you write for a paper?" I asked.

"When I was in high school, I was on the staff of my school newspaper," Dad said. "I was a reporter. So you see, I was once a writer just like you."

"Except I write books, not newspaper articles. And the ink from books doesn't rub off on your fingers."

"I never minded that," Dad said. "I loved the paper. I got to research things I wouldn't otherwise have known anything about, and I reported on people I never would've met. We had a policy at the paper to keep our stories secret from our friends, so when they read the paper they'd be learning things for the first time."

That was enough talking about newspapers for me. "I think it's time to feed the fish," I said.

Penny and I each have a pet goldfish. Mine is named Fudge, and Penny's is named Penny Jr. They both live in little glass bowls on a shelf in the kitchen.

"Can I feed one of them?" Lucy asked.

"Sure," I told her. "You can feed Penny Jr. She's the one in the bowl on the left." Penny and I usually each feed our own fish, but since she wasn't home, I figured Lucy could feed Penny Jr. this time.

"Cool, it'll be my fish for the day!" Lucy said.

Penny Jr. is pure gold—actually orange,
like the orange part of a candy corn. My fish,
Fudge, has a little fleck of black on his tail.
That's how you can tell them apart. The other
way you can tell them apart is that Fudge is a
much faster swimmer. Like right then, he was
darting all around his bowl, but Penny Jr. was

just floating in place.

"Do you think they have a secret language that they speak to each other in?" Lucy asked.

"I've never heard them make any sounds," I said. "But maybe they only do it when they know there's no one watching them."

I got the box of fish food from the pantry, and I showed Lucy how you take just a pinch of the colored flakes between your fingers, and then you sprinkle it gently on top of the water.

Fudge must have felt the water ripple, or smelled the food, or something, because he swam up to the food right away. I like to watch his mouth open up as he sucks in his flakes, like they're the yummiest things in the whole entire world, even though they kind of make your fingers smell bad when you touch them.

"Now your turn," I told Lucy.

Lucy took a pinch of flakes just like I'd showed her. She dropped them right onto the top of the water in Penny Jr.'s bowl.

"Watch her little mouth open up to grab them," I said.

But Penny Jr. didn't do anything besides just keep floating beside them.

"Hmmm," I said. "Maybe you didn't give her enough." I took another little pinch between my own fingers and dropped it in.

"Hey, that's my fish!" Lucy said. She took another pinch—this one wasn't so little—and dropped a third bit of flakes into the bowl. "Oh, Penny Jr., wake up and smell the fish flakes!"

But nothing happened except that now the top of Penny Jr.'s bowl was full of floating colored flakes, AND a floating Penny Jr.

Come to think of it, fish aren't supposed

to float, are they? They're supposed to swim.

Lucy and I realized something about Penny Jr. at the exact same time, and we looked at each other, our eyes as big and round as gumballs.

"Dad!" I cried out, so loud I heard Marco wake up and start to cry, too. "Dad!"

"What?" Dad called back.

"Come quick!" I screamed. "Something awful has happened to Penny!"

"WHAT?!" Dad screeched, and he ran to the kitchen faster than I think he'd ever run in his whole entire life.

Lucy and I were both shaking and pointing to the bowl, where Penny Jr. floated amongst the colored flakes. "She's dead!" I cried.

CHAPTER 2

Can You Keep a Secret?

"Stella, you can't do that to me," Dad said. "I thought something awful had happened to Penny."

"Something awful *did* happen to Penny," I told him.

"It was only Penny the fish," he said.

"Of course it was Penny the fish," I said. "Penny the person isn't home. But I don't think Penny the person would think it was 'only' a fish. She loved her!"

Dad took a deep breath to calm down. He stepped toward the bowl and peered closer.

"She's dead, right?" Lucy asked.

Dad nodded. "I'm afraid that happens sometimes with these little fish," he said. Marco was wailing from the other room. "Let me get the baby, and then I'll deal with it."

Lucy and I followed Dad into the living room, because suddenly we didn't want to be alone in the kitchen with Penny Jr. I wasn't sure why. The fish never scared me when it was alive. But there's something scary about dead things. Like, what if there's such a thing as a fish ghost, and now the ghost of Penny Jr. was watching us with its ghosty fish eyes. I felt shaky just thinking about it!

Dad got Marco out of his swing, and then the four of us headed back into the kitchen. Lucy wanted to hold Marco. Dad told her to sit down and use two hands, and showed her how to support his head. Then he picked up Penny Jr.'s bowl and said he'd be right back.

"Where are you going?" I asked.

"To the bathroom," Dad said. "I'll flush the fish down the toilet."

"What?!"

"It's all right, darling," Dad said. "That's what happens when a fish dies."

"But you flush the toilet when you go to the bathroom! Penny wouldn't want us to treat Penny Jr. that way!"

The phone rang just then. Dad reached over and grabbed the receiver with the hand that wasn't holding the fish bowl. "Hello?" he said. Then he paused. "Oh hi, Elaine." Elaine is my mom's name. "We're all fine, but it seems Penny's fish has moved on to a better place."

"Penny the first is going to be so sad!" I yelled toward the phone. "And Dad wants to flush Penny Jr. down the toilet!"

"Excuse me," Dad said. "I'm just going to talk to Mom privately for a sec."

I sat down across from Lucy and Marco and stuck my tongue out. Then I had to explain to Lucy I wasn't being mean, it was just Marco's new game. Soon we were all sticking our tongues out. Marco didn't know any better. He didn't know what had just happened to Penny Jr.

"We should have a funeral where we bury Penny Jr.," Lucy told me, her tongue back in her mouth. "We could do it in your backyard. That way she'll have a grave and you can always visit her."

Dad came back in and put the phone back on the cradle. "You girls okay?" he asked.

"Yup," I said.

"I've been watching Marco very carefully, Mr. Batts," Lucy added.

"Thatta girl," he said. "Just give me one more minute to take care of the fish, and then there's something I need to talk to you about."

"Wait," I said. "We need to have a funeral

for Penny Jr."

"That's very sweet," Dad said. "But we have a lot to do, and we need to do it before Penny—Penny the person—gets home."

"But Penny the person would want to say good-bye to Penny the fish," I said. "It was her fish—she's going to be the one to miss it the most. We need to call her and tell her to come home, and then we need to plan the funeral."

"That's what I want you to help me with," Dad said. "But first I need to ask, can you keep a secret?"

"I sure can, Mr. Batts," Lucy said.

"Me too," I said. "That's why you can tell me about the store."

"What about the store?" Lucy asked.

"It's nothing about the store," Dad said. "It's about the fish. Mom and I discussed it, and we both think that it would be too sad for

Penny, your sister Penny, to find out that her fish died today. So we decided to get a new one."

"But Penny won't love a new fish as much," I said.

"She will if we let her think it's the same Penny Jr. swimming around the bowl as it always was," Dad said.

"Isn't that like lying?" I asked.

"It's more like not telling the whole truth," Dad said. "Penny has been through a lot lately, with Marco coming into the family. She had to adjust to being in the middle, instead of being the littlest one. That wasn't so easy for her. You remember."

"Yeah, I remember." When Marco first came home, Penny would barely look at him. And she went around talking in a baby voice and sucking her thumb.

Goo goo ga ga go!

"Mom and I didn't have a choice in upsetting Penny with that one. Like it or not, Marco was joining our family," Dad said. "And eventually Penny did adjust and now she's just fine. But this time, maybe we can do something so Penny won't have to feel sad. We can get her a fish that looks just the same as Penny Jr. What do you say? Can you be a part of this secret mission with me, to replace Penny's fish?"

I nodded, slowly.

"Sure," Lucy said.

"But Dad, we still need to have a funeral. Penny Jr. was a member of the family."

"Okay," he said. "But we need to be quick."

We got things in order. Dad found a little

box and put Penny Jr. inside. We went to the backyard and found the perfect spot, next to a bed of flowers. I grabbed the shovel from inside the garden shed. Lucy dug a little hole. "Put the box inside," she instructed Dad. He bent down, a little awkwardly since he was holding Marco in one arm, and put the box inside the hole. Then I bent down to throw some dirt on top.

"No, not yet!" Lucy said. "I have to say some things first." She cleared her throat like a grown-up. "Ladies and gentlemen," she began. "We are gathered here today to say good-bye to our dear friend Penny Jr., who died this afternoon, just before lunchtime. It's always sad to lose a friend, but Penny Jr., we know you are swimming around freely in heaven now. And if you happen to pass by an old man with a cane who says his name is Bob

Anderson, that's my grandpop so please say hello!"

"Is that how you know so much about funerals?" I asked her. "Because of your grandpop?"

"Yup," she said. She paused. "And now it's time for YOU to say good-bye to Penny Jr."

"Uh, okay. Good-bye, Penny Jr. Fudge and I will never forget you. I hope you make a lot of fishy ghost friends." It was so weird to talk to a fish that was in a box, in the ground. "That's it."

"Now it's the dirt part," Lucy said.

We all heaped the dirt on top. Dad even let Marco have a little dirt in his hand to heap it. Mom would NOT be happy if she saw Dad let Marco touch dirt—what's dirtier than dirt?

Then it was over. We walked back to the house quietly. Except for Marco, who was crying a little bit. Even though he's just a baby, sometimes it's like he knows exactly what's going on. Maybe he was going to miss Penny Jr., too.

Good-bye, Penny Jr. You were a good fish.

CHAPTER 3

Close Calls

Even though I was sad about Penny Jr., it was kind of exciting to have a secret mission. Dad called Mom to tell her to keep Penny out of the house for at least another hour, and we drove over to Man's Best Friend. That's the pet store in the same outdoor shopping center as Batts Confections.

As we walked across the parking lot, I thought of something. "You want to protect Penny and make sure she doesn't get upset about things," I said. "I'm your daughter too, so that means you don't want me to be upset."

"I sure don't," Dad said.

"How do I know that Fudge is really Fudge, and not a new Fudge?"

"He's not," Dad said.

"You better really be telling the truth," I told him. "Because I don't want a replacement Fudge. I only want the real Fudge."

"Fudge is Fudge," Dad said.

"How can I be sure you're not lying?"

"I promise you I'm not lying."

"Do you pinky swear?" I asked.

"Pinky swear," Dad said. He shifted Marco to the side and hooked pinkies with me. "Come on, girls. If we're quick enough, we can stop by the store and you can each get a treat."

We walked into Man's Best Friend and

headed all the way to the back, to where the fish are. "Can I help you?" one of the pet store workers asked.

"We are in the market for a goldfish," Dad told him.

The man picked up his fish-scooping net. "Let me know which one you want."

Lucy and I stepped closer to the goldfish tank. "We need to find one that looks exactly like Penny Jr.," Lucy told him. "That's our fish that just died."

"My condolences," the pet store man said.

"What does 'condolences' mean?" I asked. Learning new big words is another one of my favorite things.

"It means I'm sorry for your loss," the man explained.

"Thank you," I said. "But it's not really my loss—it's my sister's. Penny Jr. was her fish, and she doesn't know that it died. So if you ever see me in here again with my sister, you have to pretend you never saw me, because this is a secret mission."

"Excuse me," a boy called from in front of a tank of tadpoles—those are the fishy things that later turn into frogs. "I need some help!"

The pet store man turned to Lucy and me. "Call me when you've settled on the one you want and I'll come back with the net. And don't worry, I'll keep your secret."

He went to help the boy, and Lucy, Dad, and I got to work studying the goldfish in the tank.

"They all look the same to me," Dad said.

"That's why it's a good thing I'm on this mission with you," Lucy said. "I'll make sure to pick the exact right Penny Jr. fish."

"It's that one over there," I said. "Right by

the blue rock. It looks so much like Penny Jr., it's probably her cousin."

Lucy shook her head. "Too shiny," she said. "Trust me. Penny Jr. was my fish for the day, so I know."

"Not a whole day," I said. "And she wasn't even alive when she was your fish. How about that one?"

"No, that one's too dull." She pointed to a fish swimming toward the top of the tank. "It's that one."

I stepped closer and traced the fish's path with my finger. I had to admit that Lucy was right: It looked so much like Penny Jr. they could be twin sisters.

We called the pet store man back over, and told him the fish we wanted. He had a plastic bag, and he first scooped some water out from the tank with a cup, so the new

Penny Jr. would have familiar water, then he used a net to scoop the fish out. It took him a couple tries because it was swimming kind of fast, but finally he captured it, and he tied up the bag with a twisty tie. "Here you go," he said. I reached for it, but Lucy said she should hold it, since technically this fish was now Penny Jr., and Penny Jr. was *still* her fish for the day.

Dad paid, and Lucy held the bag as we walked out of the pet store and into our candy store. There was still enough time to each pick a treat. "As long as you make it super snappy," Dad said.

"Oh we will," I promised, and I pulled open the big glass door that says "Batts Confections" in pink-and-silver swirly letters.

My favorite part of Batts Confections is the smell. It's a mix of chocolate and other sugary things, and now that we have the candy circus installed, there's a little bit of popcorn-y goodness mixed in.

"Hello!" Stuart called. He's my favorite person who works at our store.

"Hey, Stuart," I said, and I grabbed the fish bag from Lucy. "Meet our new fish!"

"What's this one's name?" he asked.

"Penny Jr.," I said.

"A second Penny Jr. So Penny Jr. the first . . ." Stuart's voice trailed off, and he drew his finger across his neck like he was cutting it.

"Yup," Dad said.

"I guess this one is Penny Jr. Jr. then," I told him. "But don't tell the real Penny, okay?"

"Okay," Stuart said.

"Speaking of the real Penny," Dad started, "we need to get that fish home pronto, so you and Lucy need to pick out your treats right now. Stuart, anything I should know about before we go?"

"Nope," Stuart said.

"Everything's all right up there?" Dad looked over toward the stairs that lead to the party room. At least they used to lead to the party room. Now they lead to the surprise, and there's a red rope blocking them off so people won't use them.

"Everything's fine," Stuart said.

"Wait, Stuart knows what's up there?" I asked.

"I'm telling people on a need-to-know basis," Dad said. "Stuart needs to know because he's in charge of the store when I'm not here. But you'll know soon enough."

"When?"

"On Friday. Stuart, can you do me a favor and take Marco?"

"Sure thing," Stuart said.

"Hold up, Mr. Batts, can I hold him?" Lucy asked.

"You have to pick out your treat," Dad reminded her.

"I already know what I want," Lucy said. "A Batts bar. Please, can I hold Marco? I'll use both hands, like I did before."

"I'll watch her," Stuart said.

"All right," Dad said. "Two hands, Lucy. I'm just going upstairs. I'll be right back."

While Lucy held Marco, I headed straight to the fudge counter. We always have different types of fudge to choose from. I read the choices today: chocolate, vanilla, mocha chip, M&M, cookies and cream, and on and on.

"Can I try a sliver of peanut butter swirl?" I asked Jess. She was working behind the fudge counter.

That's a rule at Batts Confections: you can taste slivers, which are eensy weensy pieces of fudge, before you decide what kind you want to buy.

Jess handed over the sliver and I sucked on it, because that's how I like to eat fudge, like I'm sucking on a hard candy. But the peanut butter was a little too sticky. I shook my head. "Nope, not this one," I said. "I think I'll have a sliver of . . . Oreo caramel, please."

Jess handed me my second sliver, and I put it on my tongue. "This is the best one," I said.

Suddenly Lucy was at my side. "And I'll have—" she started.

"You can't have any fudge," I said. "You're holding the baby and you need both hands."

"I can pick out a sliver and open my mouth and you can put it in for me," she said.

"So can I have—"

But then Stuart's voice boomed in the background. "Well hello, Batts ladies," he said. "Fancy meeting you here!"

Batts ladies?

That's what he called Penny and me—but he couldn't mean ME, because he'd already said hello. And he couldn't mean Lucy, since she's not really in our family. Which left only two Batts ladies: Mom and Penny.

Oh no, we had to hide! And quick!

I was holding Penny Jr. Jr. in one hand. With my other hand, I grabbed Lucy's arm and pulled her—and Marco—behind the fudge counter. "Girls?" Jess asked. But I put my finger to my lips and we ducked down faster than you can say "fudge sliver."

"Wah!" Marco said. Oh no! This mission was doomed. That's the problem with babies.

They don't always know what's going on, and there's no way to tell them.

But suddenly I had an idea, and I stuck my tongue out. Marco stuck his tongue out. Thank goodness. You can't cry when you're playing the tongue game.

Through the glass, I could see Stuart whispering something to Mom. "Hey, Penny," Mom said, loud enough for Lucy and me to hear, too, and even Marco, because he perked up and turned his head in the direction of Mom's voice. "Let's go downstairs to the office.

I have to pick something up."

"What?" Penny asked.

"Um," Mom hesitated for a second. "I'll show you when we get there. Come on, let's go. Now."

Marco looked like he might cry again. It didn't matter though, because now the coast was clear, and we got up from behind the counter. Stuart came over to help with Marco. He sent Jess to get Dad—which meant Jess also got to know the secret, but right then my heart was pounding too hard to care. When Dad came back, he took Marco, and we rushed outside.

"Wow," Lucy said. "That was a close one!"

"Too close," I said. "We better get into the car now." And so we did. Dad strapped Marco in, and Lucy and I buckled up by ourselves. Dad pulled out of the parking lot, and called Mom on her cell phone. He has a speakerphone in the car, so he can just say "Call Elaine," and the car knows what to do.

"Tell her we left our candy at the store by accident!" Lucy said when Mom answered.

But Mom heard. "I'm on it," she said.

Lucy had the plastic bag now, and I watched the water slosh around as Dad drove. The new Penny Jr. wasn't swimming around so much anymore. I wondered what she was thinking. Was she just done exploring or did she miss her fish friends from Man's Best Friend? She'd have another friend soon—Fudge. And I thought Fudge was the best fish in the whole entire world.

Poor Fudge. He was home all alone, and he was probably swimming around his bowl, wondering where *his* friend went. Right now the bowl next to him was empty.

Dad said good-bye to Mom. "Why are we stopped?" I asked him.

"Traffic," Dad said. "It must be the building on Camden."

"The one they're going to rename?" Lucy asked.

"That's the one," Dad said.

I reached for the fish baggie. It was probably the only time in Penny Jr.'s whole entire life that she'd be driving around in a car. It was her chance to see Somers. I was about to point out some of the sights when—

"Oh no!" I cried. I ducked my head down.

"Stella," Dad said sternly. "Don't yell while I'm driving. That's the second time you scared me today."

"But it's an emergency," I said, my head

in my lap, my body covering up Penny Jr. "Mom's car is out there—right out there next to ours."

"Where?" Lucy asked.

"Don't look," I told her. "Just duck down. Marco, duck! Duck!"

But Marco didn't know how to duck, of course, so he didn't do anything.

"You need to drive faster," I told Dad.

"I'm driving as fast as I can," he said. "Okay, I see your mother making a left, and going in the opposite direction. You can come up now, girls."

"Oh, little Penny Jr. Jr.," I said. "Your life has been full of adventures and it's just getting started."

But after that, things went exactly as planned. We got home and transferred the new Penny Jr. into the old one's bowl. She began swimming around in her fast way again—so fast that I was afraid Penny would notice she was a different fish when she came home. But then she got home, and she didn't even go into the kitchen to check on the fish.

That is, until Lucy said, "I've been taking care of Penny Jr. all day. Don't you want to say hi?"

"Yes, and, Mommy, can you come in here with our snacks? We're going into the kitchen!"

"What do you say?" Mom asked.

"Please!" Penny called.

Penny leaped up onto a chair and looked in on our fish. "Hi, Penny Jr.! Hi, Fudge!" she called. Mom walked into the room with the Batts Confections bag and handed Penny a cupcake, Lucy a Batts bar, and me a piece of Oreo caramel fudge.

"Gee, Mom, you got us exactly what we wanted," I said. "How did you know?"

"I just had a feeling," Mom said, and she winked at Lucy and me.

CHAPTER 4

Current Events

At school the next day, Mrs. Finkel announced that we were going to start a new unit. A current events unit. "Does anybody know what that is?" she asked.

A bunch of people raised their hands, including Joshua. I couldn't see him, because I'm in the front row and he's behind me. Still, I knew his hand was up because he was saying, "Oooh oooh oooh," which is the sound he makes when he raises his hand and he really

REALLY wants Mrs. Finkel to pick him.

One of Mrs. Finkel's Ground Rules is Raise Your Hand Quietly. It's posted on the board in the back. So she didn't pick him. "Yes, Clark?" she said.

"Current events are the things that are going on in the world right now."

"That is exactly right," Mrs. Finkel said. "And from now until the end of the year, two students each week will give us current events reports about what's going on right here, in Somers. Do anyone's parents get the newspaper?"

Practically everyone's hand shot up. Joshua called out, "My mom does!"

Mrs. Finkel put a finger to her lips and pointed to the list of Ground Rules. No Calling Out is also on the list. "Good," she said. "When it's your week, you should look at the local section every day, and also pay attention to the world around you. Your Thursday night homework will be writing up a summary of whatever it was that you thought was the most important thing to happen in Somers, and you'll also give a presentation to the class. Now I have everyone partnered up already—" She broke off, because Lucy was raising her hand, quietly like you're supposed to. "Yes, Lucy?" she asked.

"Can we pick our partners?" Lucy asked.

She probably wanted Talisa, because they're best friends.

"No, I made the assignments randomly, and I randomly assigned each group to a week; that's the only way to keep this fair. So let me get my list."

She bent back toward her desk and picked up a piece of paper.

"Lucy, you're actually week one, this week, with Arielle."

She was so lucky! She and Arielle were friends. Maybe not best friends, but still good friends. You could be made to be partners with someone way worse—someone like Joshua.

Mrs. Finkel went on reading. Asher was with Clark for week two. Talisa and Spencer were week three. Evie—my best friend—got to be with Maddie for week four.

Under my desk, so no one could see, I tapped my heels together three times. That's what I do when I need to make a wish. And here's what my wish was: *I really, really wish I don't get partnered up with Joshua. Please, pretty please, with a Batts Confections candied cherry on top. NO JOSHUA!*

Up to week six, which meant twelve names had been called—because that's six times two.

Not mine yet, and also not Joshua's. We have twenty-two students in our class total. There were still ten students to go.

"Okay, week seven," Mrs. Finkel said. "We have Stella—"

Oh good, I thought. *Lucky seven. And my next book would be my seventh book. So that meant I'd definitely get a good partner. And now there were nine kids left, and only one of them was Joshua. Who would it be. . . .*

"And Joshua," Mrs. Finkel finished.

What? Oh NO! How could that be? It was the complete opposite of my wish, and I'd even clicked my heels together.

"Ah, man, Smella!" Joshua said, calling out even though that's against the rules. Plus he was being mean, which isn't exactly against the rules, but it should be.

"Joshua," Mrs. Finkel said in her warning

voice. "That's enough out of you. Now to week eight."

She went on naming names, but I didn't listen. It didn't matter since my name had already been called, and I'd gotten my very last choice. Out of twenty-one other kids in my class, Joshua was the LAST person I'd ever want to be partners with for anything.

After that it was snack time. Snack is in

two parts: first you get to get up from your desk and stretch for a little bit. It's also the time when you're supposed to go to the bathroom if you have to. And then Mrs. Finkel claps her hands, which means the walking around part of snack time is over. It's time to go back to your desk and eat.

I went over to Evie's desk. That's where we all like to gather during snack. "Hey, Smella," Joshua said. "Look. Arielle's crying!"

She *was* crying, super softly so I hadn't noticed at first. But when I looked, there were tears on Arielle's cheeks, like little wet sprinkles.

Joshua talks super loudly, so now everyone was looking over at her, including Mrs. Finkel. "Arielle, is everything all right?" she asked.

"Fine," Arielle said softly. She speaks

about as softly as Joshua speaks loudly.

"Come here, please," Mrs. Finkel said. I watched her walk up to the teacher's desk. Lucy went with her.

"Stella, you come too," Lucy said.

Me? What had I done? I hadn't been the one to make Arielle cry. I hoped I wasn't about to be in trouble.

The three of us stood in front of Mrs. Finkel. "Will someone tell me what is going on?" she asked.

Arielle mumbled something that was too soft to hear. "What?" Mrs. Finkel asked. "I didn't quite catch that."

"She's afraid of presenting," Lucy spoke up.

"I understand it's a bit frightening," Mrs. Finkel said. "But you'll be speaking to your classmates, who are also your friends. My advice is to pick one person to focus on while you're talking. And then you can pretend you're just talking to him or her instead of the whole group. But you're going to have to speak up for yourself a lot of times in your life, Arielle, so it's good to practice."

"She's especially afraid of having to go the first week," Lucy went on. "So I had an idea."

Mrs. Finkel frowned and the little line between her eyebrows got a bit deeper. She didn't always like Lucy's ideas.

"Arielle can trade spots with Stella—her week one for Stella's week seven," Lucy said.

"Well," Mrs. Finkel began.

"You don't mind, Stella, do you?" Lucy asked.

I shook my head. "I don't. But then . . ." I trailed off.

"Then what?"

"Then Arielle would have to be with Joshua, and that wouldn't be fair."

"I don't mind," Arielle said, her voice soft as usual. As soft as cotton candy on your tongue.

"She'd rather be with a meanie than go first," Lucy explained. "And Stella doesn't want to be with him at all. So it's perfect."

We looked over at Mrs. Finkel. I was afraid she was about to be mad that we'd called Joshua a meanie. "You know, when I made these pairs," she said, "I thought it might be good for Stella and Joshua to work together. But because of his outburst today—I know that wasn't your fault, Stella, and I know that makes this project a bit more difficult for you. Do you understand what I'm saying?"

I understood: If she were me, she wouldn't want to be partners with Joshua, either. I nodded.

"So I'm going to say yes to this change. But that's it. No more trading."

I smiled—my wish had come true! It just took a little while, but maybe some wishes are like that.

"Great!" Lucy said. She turned to Arielle. "Now do you mind going away for a minute? I need to ask Mrs. Finkel something in private."

"Sure," Arielle said.

I started to walk away with her, but Lucy stopped me. "You can stay, Stella. You're my partner now." She waited until Arielle had walked back to her desk, and then she said, "Can we make our own newspaper to hand out to the class?"

"You can do whatever you want, as long as you also give a presentation."

"Yay!" Lucy said. Then she lowered her voice. "Yay," she said more softly. "It's okay if a grown-up helps us with the typing part, right?"

"Of course."

"Good. Stella's dad will help us, because he knows a lot about newspapers."

"I just have to ask him first," I said.

"One more thing," Lucy told Mrs. Finkel.

"It's okay if we don't tell anyone else yet, right? I want it to be a surprise. Like your dad said, Stella. We'll keep the stories secret so when our friends read them, they'll be learning something new."

"That's a great idea," I said.

"Do you pinky swear that you'll keep the secret?" Lucy asked me.

I held out my pinky and hooked it onto Lucy's. "Pinky swear," I said.

"And you too, Mrs. Finkel?" Lucy asked.

Mrs. Finkel didn't hold up a pinky, but she nodded. "Your secret is safe with me."

CHAPTER 5

None of Your Beeswax

At lunch, Lucy squeezed in between Evie and me, instead of sitting across from us, next to Talisa, the way she normally does. "I think we should sit together because of you-know-what," she said.

"What?" Evie asked.

"Our current events project," I replied.

"Shhh," Lucy warned.

"Don't worry," I said. "I won't tell the secret part—but it's not a secret that we're doing a project together. Arielle already knows."

"I thought you and Arielle were doing it together," Talisa said.

"We traded," Lucy said.

"I didn't know you could trade. I want to trade. I'm with a boy!"

"But you're with Spencer," I said. "He's a nice boy."

"We're the only ones allowed to trade," Lucy said. "Now we really can't tell you anymore."

Talisa was frowning. So was Evie. "Let's talk on the phone after school," I said.

"I have tap class after school," Lucy said. "But I can call you after that. Or maybe we should each read the paper first, before we talk. So I'll call you after dinner, at seven-thirty?"

"That's great," I said. "So you'll read and

I'll read, and I'll also talk to my dad about . . . about that other thing."

"What other thing?" Evie asked.

"None of your beeswax," Lucy said.

"That's mean!" Evie said. "You'll tell me, won't you, Stella?"

"Stella can't say anything," Lucy said. "She pinky-sweared."

I shook my head. "Sorry, it's true. I can't."

"Aw, come on," Talisa said.

"EWWWWWWW!" someone cried from the table next to us, and we all turned to look. It was Asher who'd yelled. He's not usually a yeller. He's not quiet, like Arielle is. He just talks in a normal voice most of the time.

Now he was standing up, and so were all the other boys at their table. All the boys, except for Joshua.

"Can someone help?" Asher called. "Joshua threw up!"

"I'd hate to throw up in school," Arielle said softly.

I would, too. But there was a part of me that was glad about Joshua—because he'd called me Smella before, the way he always does, and now he was the one who did the gross thing.

Also no one was thinking about Lucy's and my secret anymore, and that was good, too.

At 7:30 on the dot, the phone rang. "It's for me!" I shouted. "I know it's for me!" But then it stopped ringing, and no one called to me to say pick up the phone. So maybe it was someone else who was calling at exactly 7:30. What if Mom or Dad was still on the phone when Lucy called? I had to tell them it was important that I talk to Lucy right away. Otherwise they might take a message and it could get too late.

I walked into the kitchen where Dad was cleaning up from dinner. He had the cordless

phone balanced between his shoulder and his ear.

"Dad," I said. "If Lucy calls . . ."

He turned around from the sink and held up a soapy finger to signal, *just one sec.*

"She's right here, Lucy," he said. "Hold on. Stel, can you take the phone from me?"

I stood on my tiptoes and Dad bent down a little. "Hello," I said into the receiver. "I have so much to tell you, but first I need to go to my room for privacy."

"Oh, good idea," Lucy said.

I ran down the hall, into my room, and closed the door. "Okay," I said. "Hello again."

"Hello. I just talked to your dad and he said he's going to help with our project!"

"That's what I was going to tell you," I said. "I asked him earlier and he said he can be our typer, and he even said he has his old newspaper program on the computer at the store, and we can go there after school on Thursday and use it."

"Yeah, he told me that too," Lucy said.

"Did he tell you his tips for being a reporter?" I asked.

"No, he didn't get to that part because you walked in."

"Don't worry," I said. "I can tell you now. He said a reporter always carries a notebook with her, in case you observe anything important, or want to write down something someone said. Also, the more questions you ask, the more you know. And the more you know, the better your story will be."

"I knew that already," Lucy said.

"I thought you said he didn't get to tell you his pointers."

"Yeah, but I just knew them."

"Oh. Did you read the paper today?"

"I did."

"Did you see anything exciting? I didn't."

"I didn't either. But I have some ideas. How's Penny doing with her new fish?"

"She's okay," I whispered.

"What?"

"I can't talk about it," I said. "In case she hears."

"We need a code," Lucy said. "We'll call it PB."

"What does that mean?"

"Private business," Lucy said. "That's the secret code I made up. In case we need to talk about things and we don't want anyone to know. Get it?"

"I got it," I said.

CHAPTER 6

Some Things Are Too Personal

At home I read the newspaper every morning with Dad.

I read an article about our mayor. It gave lots of details about her, like where she went to school, and how she works to keep our bay clean, and that she is a vegetarian. Dad said someone must've interviewed her to get all the details. She seemed like a nice person and a good mayor. Still, I was looking for something else for my presentation.

I kept reading the paper. Here are more things I read about:

1. New trees being planted at City Hall (trees are good to look at, but not so fun to write about)

2. A bunch of sporty things (I like gymnastics the best, but the sports were different teams like football and soccer)

3. A new recycling program at Somers High School (but I go to Somers Elementary School)

I paid attention to stuff around me, looking for interesting things that affected my life. So far the most interesting thing was that Joshua wasn't in school on Tuesday, or on Wednesday. It affected my life because no one called me Smella, but it wasn't the kind of thing I could write about, either.

At snack time on Wednesday, we were

standing around Evie's desk, just like usual. "We" means me, Arielle, Talisa, Lucy, and Evie, of course. Except Evie was sitting.

"I bet Mrs. Finkel is happy Joshua is absent," Lucy said. "She hasn't had to yell at anyone for disobeying the Ground Rules all week. When she goes home at night, she probably hopes he stays sick!"

I knew it was sort of a mean thing for Lucy to say, but I think she was right. The thing about Lucy is she always tells the truth, even if the truth is not that nice.

"What else do you think Mrs. Finkel does when she's at home?" Talisa asked.

"She takes care of Evan and Shadow," I said.

"Who?" Evie asked.

"Her son and her dog," I said.

"Mrs. Finkel has a son and a dog?"

"Yup, I saw them once."

I hadn't told anyone about meeting Evan and Shadow, because right after was when Evie's dog, Bella, got lost. But now I told them. They were all really interested. They wanted to know more.

That was when I knew exactly what I wanted to do for my article. "Hey, Lucy!" I said. "I just had the best . . ."

"What?" Evie asked.

Oops.

"Never mind. I'll tell you later."

"Is it about our PB?" Lucy asked.

I nodded.

"What's PB?" Evie asked.

"It's a code," I started to explain.

"Shhh," Lucy said.

"Knock, knock," Talisa said.

"Who's there?" we all asked.

"You," Talisa said.

"You who?" we asked.

"Yoo-hoo, I wish you would tell me what you're talking about!"

"You'll see," Lucy told her.

"Will you sit with me for lunch today, Stella?" Evie asked.

"She has to sit with me," Lucy told her.

"I have two sides," I said. "Lucy can sit on one and you can sit on the other."

Evie shook her head. "Not if you and Lucy are going to be talking about your BP the whole time. Then it's not fun to sit next to you."

"PB," Lucy corrected.

"Whatever," Evie said. She looked upset.

"We won't talk about it," I promised.

Then Mrs. Finkel clapped her hands, which meant the talking part of snack was over. I went back to my desk and pulled out my apple slices and the eensy weensy piece of fudge Mom had packed for snack. But before I started eating, I had to speak to Mrs. Finkel.

I raised my hand.

"Yes, Stella?" Mrs. Finkel said.

"Can I come up to your desk?"

"Sure."

I stood up. Down the row, Lucy's hand shot up. "Excuse me, Mrs. Finkel?" she said.

"Yes, Lucy?"

"Can I come too? I think Stella wants to talk about . . . about our PB."

"I'm not sure what that is," Mrs. Finkel said. "But yes, you can both come up."

Lucy met me up at Mrs. Finkel's desk. "That's what this is about, right? PB?"

"Yup," I said.

"I can only assume that has something to do with your project," Mrs. Finkel said.

"Yes," I told her. I lowered my voice to just above a whisper, like the way Arielle talks in her regular voice. "I know what I want to do for my article, and I was wondering—could I ask you a few questions for it?"

"Go ahead."

"Oh," I said. "I can't ask you all my questions right now. There are too many people and I want it to be a surprise." Even though I was whispering, the rest of the room was quiet, so kids could still hear me.

"How about if we step into the hallway for a second?" Mrs. Finkel said. I nodded and she stood up from her desk. "Clark?" she called. "I'm going to be just outside. Can you be the classroom monitor for a couple minutes while I step outside?"

"Yes, Mrs. Finkel," Clark said.

Lucky! He got picked to be class monitor. But of course I couldn't be, because I was going to step outside with Mrs. Finkel.

"Come up here and sit at my desk, so you can watch your classmates," Mrs. Finkel told him. "And everyone else, I expect good behavior. I'm not going far."

I followed her out into the hallway. Lucy came too, even though it was my PB.

"Oops, I forgot my notebook."

I dashed back into the room and grabbed my notebook, and a pencil too. I knew everyone was looking at me as I ran back into the hall. "So, Stella," Mrs. Finkel said. "I'm still not sure what this is about."

"Me either," said Lucy.

"I want to interview you," I told her.

"About what?" asked Mrs. Finkel.

"About you," I told her. "You said we should write about a subject that affects us, and of course you affect us, because you're our teacher and we see you every day. But all we know is what happens in the classroom. We don't know what you do when you get home, what your hobbies are. The more you know about something, the better. And I know

the rest of the class would be interested in it. You're like the mayor of our class."

"Well, Stella," said Mrs. Finkel. "I'm very flattered that you think your classmates would find an article about me interesting, but this wasn't exactly what I had in mind for this project."

"But you told us it was okay if our project was a little bit different," Lucy reminded her.

"That's not exactly what I said," Mrs. Finkel said. "What I said was you could print your articles out like a real newspaper. But that's not the problem. The problem is that I'm your teacher, yes, so things that happen in this classroom affect you and your classmates. But what happens outside of this classroom is my private life. Do you understand what I'm saying?"

Yes, she was saying None of Your Beeswax.

"All right, I think it's time for geography. Let's head back inside," Mrs. Finkel said.

Back inside meant I had NO project.

⊙

After school, Mrs. Benson drove our carpool home. She's Zoey's mom, and Zoey is

Penny's best friend.

"I really can't wait until Friday when your project is over," Evie told me. She's also in our carpool.

"Yeah, me too," I said. It wasn't even fun anymore.

"You can just tell me what the secret is," Evie said.

"There's a secret?" Penny asked.

"Who has a secret?" asked Zoey.

"Stella does," Evie said. "But you can trust me with it, Stella. I won't tell anyone. I'm your best friend in Somers."

"And I'm your sister," Penny added.

"And I'm your sister's best friend," said Zoey.

I shook my head. "I can't tell," I said. "No one knows."

"Lucy does," said Evie.

"Well, it's her secret, too," I told her.

Mrs. Benson pulled up in front of our house. "All right, Batts girls," she said. "Up and out!"

Penny and I unbuckled our seat belts and climbed out of the car. Dad was at the front door waiting for us. He waved to Mrs. Benson, Zoey, and Evie, and then they drove away.

"Where's Mom?" I asked.

"She's at the store," Dad said. "I decided to stay home with Marco."

"Stella has a secret," Penny complained, as we kicked off our shoes in the front hall.

"So do I," Dad said.

"We know," I said. "The secret at the store. You won't tell us."

"And it's not fair," Penny added.

"Well," Dad said. "If you girls promise not to say anything, I will tell you all about it."

CHAPTER 7

Dad's Secret

But Dad didn't tell us right away. First we fed our fish while Dad made us a snack.

"Look how swimmy my fish is," Penny said. "I think she's growing up and getting more energy. Like how Marco used to sleep more when he was a little baby, but now he's more awake."

"Marco is sleeping now," I pointed out.

"Yeah, but not as much as he used to. Just like Penny Jr."

I nodded. I was afraid to talk because what if I accidentally told Penny the truth about Penny Jr. Jr. Having a secret is hard work. You have to be very careful about what you say and what you don't say.

Dad gave us apple slices. "That's it?" Penny asked. "That's not fair! Mom always lets us have something sweet along with something healthy."

"The sweet snack will come later, along with a surprise," Dad told her.

"I don't like surprises," I told him. "I like knowing things."

"You'll know soon enough," Dad told me. "After you eat something healthy, and do your homework. You both have homework, right?"

"Yup," said Penny. "We're doing our letters right now. I'm supposed to write out the whole alphabet—uppercase and lowercase.

And then I have to practice the sounds."

"And what about you, Stel?" Dad asked.

"I have to read the paper, which I already did with you this morning. I have a math worksheet that I finished this afternoon in free period. So all I have to do is work on my article."

"Great," Dad said.

Penny and I finished our apples and stood up. "Bye, little fishies," Penny called. "I love you, Penny Jr. And I love you too, Fudge—but not as much."

Then we went to our rooms to do our homework. I sat at my desk to work on my article, even though I didn't have a topic yet.

Sometimes, when I'm working on my books, I just write whatever pops into my head. I decided to try that with my report:

I wish I could tell you about the mayor of our class, Mrs. Finkel. But she didn't want me to.

I scrunched up the paper. She'd probably get mad about that.

I'd read about the heat wave in the paper that morning. That affected my life because it was hot. So I tried that:

The weather is hotter than usual in Somers this week. That affects my life because I don't have to wear a sweater.

Just then I heard a knock. "Who is it?" I called.

"It's Penny."

"Come in," I said.

Penny skipped into my room with her

notebook. "Look, I finished all my letters. I think it was my neatest handwriting ever."

I looked. It was neat—for a kindergartener.

"I have to practice sounding out things too," Penny said. "Did you write anything in your book? Can I sound it out?"

"My books are private," I told her.

"How about if I read your homework then?" she asked. She leaned over my shoulder. "The www . . . www."

"Weather," I told her.

"Oh, that's a hard word," she said. "But I can read the little ones. And I can read my whole name—Penelope."

"That's good," I told her.

"You're writing about the weather for your homework?"

"Nope." I scrunched up the paper. I still

had a couple days to work on it. "I'm done for now."

"Goody! It's surprise time! Come on, let's go!" Penny said.

Penny and I walked into the living room.

"Ready to go?" Dad asked.

"Where are we going?"

"The store," he said.

"Is Marco coming too?" I asked.

"Of course," Dad said. "We can't leave him here on his own."

On the ride over, Penny was going through a list of treats she thought maybe she'd like to have: jump rope jellies, and every color of M&M, and glow-in-the-dark bubble gum.

"Penny," I said. "The treats aren't a surprise. I think Dad's going to tell us what's upstairs."

"Don't ruin it, Stel," Dad said.

"I can't ruin it! I don't know what it is—but I can't wait to find out!"

When we got to the store, Mom came upstairs and Dad handed Marco over. "We'll meet you at home in an hour or so, is that all right?" he asked.

"That's just fine," Mom said. "Marco and I will get dinner started." She kissed us all good-bye. "You girls be careful, all right?" Mom said.

"We will," Penny said.

I nodded, but something was weird. We'd been in the store about a million bazillion times before, and she'd never told us to be careful. "Is there something dangerous up there?" I asked.

"Oh no!" Penny cried. "Is it a snake? Or is it a clown???"

"Calm down," Dad said. "It's nothing scary. I'll show you in a second, but I need you to promise me that you won't tell anyone what I'm about to show you."

Penny and I both promised. Dad walked over and lifted the red rope by the stairs. Penny and I climbed under. Then Dad climbed over the rope, because he's tall and his legs are long enough to do that. He moved ahead of us. At the top of the steps, he pulled aside a plastic curtain.

"Come on, girls, you can come in."

The upstairs is one big room. The floor was covered in brown paper, the kind of paper you wrap around boxes to ship them out. There were wires hanging down from the ceiling, and from a few places on the walls. One whole wall wasn't a wall at all. It was just pink soft stuff. Like a pink cloud, or a pillow, or ... or ... "Hey, that looks like cotton candy!" I said.

"Ooh, cool," Penny said. She reached out a hand to touch it, but Dad pulled her back.

"That's insulation," he said. "The wall hasn't been put up yet. Stay close to me, okay? Just around here."

We stepped around a ladder, and some other things that I couldn't tell what they were because there were big white sheets draped over them. But I could tell they weren't the table and chairs that used to be in the room, because the shapes were different. Also BIG. There were splashes of paint everywhere—on

the sheets and on the floor. And against the far wall, big stripes of color: purple, orange, green, pink, yellow, blue.

"This is the surprise?" Penny asked.

Dad nodded. "Remember the leak?" he asked.

"No," Penny said.

"I remember," I said. "It was right before we left to go to Aunt Laura's wedding. But I didn't think it was this bad."

"It wasn't this bad, Stel," Dad said. "Just one spot on the ceiling that dripped down the far wall. But it was enough that we had to repaint this room, and it got me thinking. . . . Maybe it was time for a change up here."

"Like we changed the downstairs?" Penny asked. "When you changed the candy garden to a candy circus?"

"Exactly," he said. "We've had the castle

party room theme for quite awhile. I had an idea for this room that I wasn't sure would work, but Mom and I discussed it, and decided it was worth a try. Any guess before I tell you what it is?"

"A party room set up to look like the dining room at a fancy party—like at Aunt Laura's wedding?" I asked.

"Nope, guess again," Dad said.

"A pirate ship?" Penny asked.

"A pirate ship?" I asked. "That doesn't make any sense."

"It doesn't not make sense," she said. "There could be hidden treasure under the sheets. And look at that—that's tall enough to be the sail."

"That's true," Dad said. "But that's not what it is either. Do you give up?" Penny and I both said we did. Dad told us to stand back and he whipped off one of the sheets. "Voila!" he said.

Underneath was the last thing I expected to see—a slide! The slide part itself was yellow, like a lemon ball, and there were white stairs leading up to the top. It wasn't that tall, but it did have a twisty middle, which made it cooler than a plain, regular slide.

"Wow, can we use it?" Penny asked.

"Sure," Dad told her. "You'll be the first. But here, you'll need these." He dug a couple coins out of his pocket, and handed them to Penny. She turned them over in her hands. "Can you read what it says?" Dad asked.

"It says Batts!" she said.

"It can't say Batts," I told her.

"Yes, it does," Penny said. "I know that word by heart. I don't even have to sound it out when I see it. Here, look."

She handed one over.

"Wow, it *does* say Batts. Can you buy things with it?"

"Right there," Dad said, pointing. For the first time, I noticed the money slot by the stairs leading up to the slide.

"Insert two tokens," I read out loud.

"What's a token?" Penny asked.

"It's what you have in your hand," Dad said. "A special coin made up just for the store, for these activities. Go on, try it out."

Penny put her token in, and I put mine in, and all of a sudden there was a dinging noise and the little lights started flashing on the stairs, in all different colors, like suddenly there were M&Ms or Skittles popping up.

"Whoa," Penny said.

"Go on up," Dad said. "Try it out."

Penny climbed up the steps and slid down. "Whee!" she called. "Hey, what's this?" she asked, when she got to the bottom. It looked like some sort of pedal, and she could reach it with her foot when she was sitting at the end of the slide.

"Press it," Dad told her.

Penny did, and there was a mechanical noise and then out came tickets from a slot right by the side of the slide.

Penny ripped them off. "I got three!" she said. "Three tickets!" She paused. "But what do I do with them?"

"I bet I know," I said. "Kids can come up here and play a bunch of games, like at an arcade, and then they get a bunch of tickets. And probably they can use those tickets to get candy downstairs."

"You got it, Stel," Dad said. "From now on, whoever comes to Batts Confections will have a choice. They can pay with money downstairs, or they can come up here, play some games, collect a few tickets, and then go down to make their selection. Mom, Stuart, and I are working on how many tickets you'll need for each treat downstairs. Like for example, three tickets will probably buy you a Marco's Mini."

"So you can slide down the slide a bunch of times and get more than three tickets and buy more Marco's Minis," Penny said.

"Right," Dad said. We stepped around some planks of wood and buckets of paint. Dad lifted up the sheets to show us the things underneath them, like skee ball. That's a game where you get a bunch of balls, and you have to toss them so they roll up a hill, and try to

get them to land in the holes at the top. The closer you are to the center hole, the more tickets you get. There was also a basketball game, a strong-man game, a ring-toss game, and even a little miniature-golf game. You had to putt the golf ball through a hole.

Dad let me test out the miniature-golf game. It looked easy, but it wasn't because the hole was eensy weensy. It took me five putts to get the ball in, and then I had three tickets, too.

"We'll have picnic benches up here too," Dad said. "So adults can sit down while they supervise."

"Cool," I said.

"I like the rainbow on the wall," Penny said.

"Actually," Dad told her, "those are just sample colors, to figure out what to paint the walls. Any favorites?"

"I like purple," I said. "And yellow and blue."

"Me too," Penny said, copying me. "And also pink."

"Well, we have four walls, and those are four colors," Dad said. "We can use them all."

"Goody!" Penny said.

"But what about Marco?" I asked.

"He's too little for a favorite color," Penny said. "That's why it's good to be big!"

Dad smiled at her. "By the time he's big enough, who knows what changes we'll be making at Batts Confections," he said.

"And I'll be even bigger," Penny said.

"And I'll be even bigger than that," I told her. "But I still have a question. The kids who come in here to play the games—where do they get the tokens?"

"Aha!" Dad said. "I was waiting for you to ask me that." He stepped over to one more thing covered in a thick white sheet and pulled it off. "Here!" he said.

It was a token machine, like at a real arcade. You put a dollar in and four of the special Batts Confections tokens came out. "Can I do it?" I asked.

"Can I do it too?" Penny asked.

Dad shook his head. "There will be plenty of time for you to get Batts Confections tokens in the future. For now we need to clean up and head home." We helped him pull the sheets back over the games and the token machine. That way, when they painted the room, they wouldn't get dripped on. Then we headed downstairs to say good-bye to Stuart, and also to trade in our tickets for treats. I got a piece and a half of fudge. The whole piece was buttercream-birthday-cake-frosting fudge and the half was red-velvet fudge. Penny got three things from the Penny Candy Wall.

In the car on the way home, Dad told us there was going to be an article about the new candy arcade in the paper on Friday. Until then it was a secret. "And I know I can trust you girls with it."

"When we get home I'm going to write about it for my article," I said.

"But it's a secret!" Penny said. "Dad just said so."

"I know," I said. "I'm just going to write about it now. I'm not going to show anyone what I've written until Friday. I won't even show Lucy until then. We have our presentation on Friday, and that's when I'm allowed to tell people, right?"

"Right," Dad said.

"Then kids will find out about it and want to go, and we'll get even more business."

"Now that sounds like a great idea."

CHAPTER 8

Thursday

School wasn't so much fun on Thursday. At snack, the only person who talked to me was Lucy. And at lunch, Talisa and Evie said they were going to have a Spit Tournament. Spit is our favorite card game. I don't know why it's called that, because it actually doesn't have anything to do with saliva.

"Can I play winner?" Lucy asked.

"No, Arielle gets to," Talisa said.

"And after that?"

Talisa shook her head. "We're only doing two rounds for the tournament," she said.

"I think they're mad at us," I told Lucy. "Because of the PB."

"You can't tell them," Lucy said.

"I know," I said.

But I hadn't realized people would get upset, back when I'd told Lucy I'd keep it a secret. The thing is, once you promise to keep a secret, you can't go back on it.

"Do you have your article ready for later?" Lucy asked me.

"Yes, I do. But I can't tell you what it's about."

"Hold up," Lucy said. "You're allowed to tell *me* your PB."

"I can't tell you this," I said. "I promised. You'll find out tomorrow with everyone else."

"Then I'm not going to tell you what

mine is about," she said.

"Fine."

"Fine. Only your dad will know both, because he's doing the typing. And I'll make sure he doesn't tell you, either."

After school we went outside to the flagpole, where Dad was waiting for us. Penny was going home with Zoey—the kindergarteners get out five minutes earlier than the rest of us, so she wasn't even there. Evie, who usually carpools with us, had a playdate with Arielle.

I had plans with Lucy, which is different from a playdate. She came in the car with Dad and me. We told him the deal we'd made: that when he was typing up Lucy's article, I would help Stuart behind the register. And when he was typing up my article, Lucy would help Stuart.

"Just one kink in the plan," said Dad. "Stuart's going to do the typing because I'll be upstairs working on—"

"Please don't tell Lucy what that is," I interrupted Dad. "We're not sharing articles."

"Gotcha," he said.

"Hold up, Mr. Batts," Lucy said. "We need you to help us make the newspaper."

"I will," Dad said. "Stuart will just do the typing."

"And we can trust him with what our articles are about, and he won't tell anyone?"

"He won't tell a soul," Dad promised. "Stuart's the most trustworthy guy I know."

Dad pulled the car into the parking lot. It was pretty crowded, which meant we had to park farther away, which Dad says is good exercise, even though I like parking close. That way we can get into the store—and to the candy—even faster.

We did Rock, Paper, Scissors to see who would go first, and Lucy won. She and Stuart went downstairs to type up her article. Dad went upstairs to check out the painting of the walls of the you-know-what.

Jess was working at the fudge counter, and she said I could help her. I love working at

the fudge counter because you get three jobs:

 Cutting people slivers of flavors they want to taste.

2. Weighing the fudge that they pick.

3. Working the cash register.

But I only got to help out two customers, because then Lucy came back upstairs and said it was my turn to go have Stuart type up my article. I grabbed my backpack and headed to Dad's office downstairs. Stuart was waiting for me at the computer. "Step right up!" he said.

I did, but then suddenly I squeezed my eyes shut. "Wait, that's not Lucy's article on the screen right now, is it? Because I'm not allowed to see it."

"Nope, don't worry," Stuart said. "It's just a blank screen. I'm ready to type up whatever you've got."

I pulled my notebook out of my backpack, flipped open to my article, and handed it over. "Do you want me to read it to you?"

"Nope, I can touch-type," Stuart said.

"What does that mean? Aren't you always touching the keys if you're typing?"

"That sounds like what it should mean, but really it means that I know exactly where the keys are on the keyboard, so I can type without looking at it. So I can read what you've written and type it up at the exact same time."

It was almost like learning a new big word, even though it was really two words: touch and type.

"Here, watch," Stuart said. He propped my notebook up right next to the screen and began typing:

This article is going to be about an

exciting new thing happening at Batts Confections. In case you don't know, that's my family's candy store. It affects my life because it's where my parents work. It also affects other people in Somers, because they like to visit and buy lots of sweets.

Stuart went on for three more paragraphs and never even looked down at his fingers! And he was super fast, too. We were all done in five minutes. Stuart took me back up to the first floor. He called Dad's cell phone. Lucy and I worked at the cash register until Dad came down. "Hey, Mr. Batts, you have paint on your shirt!" Lucy said.

"Shhh!" I said. "Don't tell her why."

"Don't worry," Dad said, "I'll never tell."

"Until tomorrow," I added.

The three of us went downstairs together to make our articles look like a newspaper. Except we couldn't look at the screen when Dad was doing it, or we'd see each other's articles. I squeezed my eyes shut tight.

"Wait," Dad said. "What about the finished product? Won't you both see that?"

"I was thinking about that, Mr. Batts,

and I think I have a solution," Lucy told him. I opened one of my eyes up an eensy weensy bit, just to make sure hers were still closed tight. They were. "You're the one who has to make it look like a newspaper. So when you're all done, you can print the copies out. Twenty-two copies for all the kids in our class."

"And one more for Mrs. Finkel," I added.

"Right, twenty-three total. And then you can put them in an envelope and seal it up. Stella can bring it to school, but she can't open it without me!"

"I won't," I said. "I pinky swear." I reached out to find Lucy's hand, and hooked my pinky on hers.

"Okay," Lucy said. "And Mr. Batts, one more thing. Put 'PB' on the envelope. That's our code, and then we'll know what it is, but no one else will."

"Print them out, put in envelope, seal it up, and write 'PB'—and that stands for what?"

I started to answer, but then Dad cut me off. "Never mind. You don't have to tell me any secrets."

"Thanks for understanding, Mr. Batts," Lucy said.

Dad turned back to the computer. I could tell because I could hear his fingers click-clacking on the keyboard, even though my eyes were closed and I couldn't see him. But then his phone rang.

"Hi, Stuart," Dad answered. He paused. "Yes, I'm down here with the girls still, but I can come up."

There were a couple more click-clacks. Then Dad said, "You can open your eyes." We did. "According to Stuart, I'm needed upstairs on the super secret project going on up there,

131

and I don't know how long it's going to take. So I think I'll have Stuart take you home now. When I'm finished upstairs, I'll format it all out, as promised."

"But, Dad, we wanted to watch you," I said.

"You girls have your eyes squeezed shut," he reminded me.

We went back upstairs. Jess let Lucy and me each have a piece of fudge—and I took one extra piece for Penny, and Lucy took one extra piece for her sister, Ann. Dad said good-bye to us. Stuart drove Lucy home first, and then he drove me.

By the time Penny and I were getting ready for bed, Dad still hadn't come home.

But he called to say goodnight to Penny and me, and even Marco—he can't talk, but Mom had Dad on speakerphone. Marco didn't say anything back, of course. He just drooled.

"I'll see you in the morning," Dad said.

"Wait!" Penny cried. "You didn't say goodnight to Belinda!"

"Goodnight, Belinda," said Dad.

"No, she's not here," Penny said. "Hold on, I'll go get her." And she took off down the hall.

"Don't forget to put 'PB' on the envelope," I said while we were waiting for her to come back.

"PB?" Mom asked.

"It's a secret," Dad told her. "And don't worry, Stel, I won't."

Then Penny was back, and she held Belinda up to the phone, and said, "Goodnight,

Grandpa," in her baby voice. (According to Penny, Belinda is her baby, which makes Belinda Dad's *grand*baby.)

"Goodnight, everyone!" Dad said. "See you tomorrow."

I went to bed soon after that. Usually I read a book for a half hour before I go to sleep. But instead, I pulled my notebook out of my backpack to read my article over again, since I'd have to get up in front of the whole entire class the next day and talk about it. Everyone would be looking at me, and listening to me, and . . .

Uh oh. Arielle was right: It was going to be scary!

I fell asleep and dreamed that I was standing in front of the classroom, but instead of twenty-one other kids staring back at me, it was like a thousand. And they weren't in our classroom. They were in a huge concert hall—like the one on Camden Road. Except it didn't have a ceiling. It was just a wide-open space and I was flying above, through the air. I flapped my arms and tried to get back to the ground, but I just went higher. That's when I started to scream.

My eyes popped open, but the screaming went on and on.

"AHHHHHHHHHHHHHHH!"

CHAPTER 9

Everyone Finds Out

"AHHHHHHHHHHHH!" Penny screamed.

Oh no! Was she hurt? Was she in trouble?

My heart was already thump-thumping in my chest from the scariest dream. I felt wide awake, and I jumped out of bed and started to run down the hall. "Penny, I'm coming!" I called.

She was standing in the hallway, just by the front door. Mom was next to her. Dad was there, too. He was bent down, with Marco in one arm, gathering up a bunch of papers on the floor with his free hand.

When Dad stood up, I could see Marco making his getting-ready-to-cry face. Soon he started wailing. I'm pretty sure he thinks it's a rule that if someone else is crying, he's supposed to cry, too.

Mom held a tissue up to Penny. "Take a deep breath. Blow your nose and wipe your face. It's going to be okay."

"What happened?" I asked.

"She knows about the fish," Dad said. He'd put the papers on the hall table, and now he was jiggling Marco up and down in his arms. Marco stopped crying and started hiccupping.

"How?" I asked.

"I read it!" Penny said. "In the newspaper!"

"There was an article about Penny's fish

in the newspaper? And Penny read it? But she can't even read."

Penny sniffled loudly. "I can so read!" she said. "I've been practicing lots and lots! But now I'm never going to read ever again!"

"Now, now, Pen," Mom said.

"It was in *your* newspaper," Dad explained. He nodded toward the pile of papers on the hall table. "I left the envelope on the counter and Penny opened it up."

I stepped over and saw the headline at the top of the page: *How Penny Jr. Died and It Affected My Life.* So that was what Lucy's article was about! "But I thought you put it in an envelope and sealed it up and wrote 'PB' on it."

"Those are my initials," Penny said.

"It was supposed to stand for Private Business, not Penny Batts," I said. "That meant none of your beeswax."

"Stella," Dad said. "Now is not the time for that kind of behavior. Do you have anything to say to your sister?"

"Sorry, Penny," I said. "We should have picked a different code."

"I don't think that's what matters right now," Mom said. "What matters is that Penny is sad about her fish."

"How come everyone knew what happened except for me, and she was all mine?! I should've known what happened to her!"

"You're right, Penny," Dad said. "We shouldn't have kept this from you. From now on, we won't have any secrets when it comes to your fish. I promise."

"I promise too," Mom told her. "The truth is, Penny Jr. died a few days ago. That's when your dad and I—and Stella—decided to get you a new fish."

"That part wasn't in Lucy's article?" I asked.

"I didn't read too far," Penny said, crying again. "It was too hard and too sad."

Marco started to cry again too, even though Dad was doing a lot of jiggling. "I think we should feed this little guy," Dad said.

"And I think we should feed you girls," Mom said. She took Penny's hand. "I know it's really sad when something you love dies. Penny Jr. was a good little fish and we'll always remember her. But there's a new fish in the kitchen that you've been loving all week long, and *still* needs your love and attention."

"Its name is Penny Jr. Jr.," I added. "And it looks so much like the first Penny Jr., we think they were probably twins, or at least cousins."

But when we got into the kitchen, Penny wouldn't even look at Penny Jr. Jr., and I had to feed both fish by myself. Dad handed the baby over to Mom and he got to work making pancakes—Penny's favorite breakfast. "Come on, Pen, you'll help me make the shapes," he said.

Usually Penny is good at being distracted. But right then she was so upset about the fish, it wasn't working. When the pancakes were done, she didn't eat much. I knew just how she was feeling. When Evie's dog, Bella, got lost, I missed her so much, and it made me not hungry at all.

After breakfast we did the usual get-ready stuff, like brush teeth and get dressed. I took the pile of newspapers Dad made and put them back into the "PB" envelope. I put the envelope into my backpack and put on my

shoes. Then Mrs. Benson honked her horn.

"But I thought Mr. King was driving carpool today," I said as we got in the car.

"Evie's dad called me this morning to say he had an errand, and he asked if we could trade days."

"What about Evie?"

"He's taking her to school on the way.

You'll see her in class."

I wondered if that was the real reason Evie didn't drive with us. Or maybe she didn't drive with us because she didn't want to be in the same car as me—because she was mad at me about all the secrets.

We pulled up in front of school. "Goodbye, girls," Mrs. Benson said.

I got to our classroom just as Mrs. Finkel was about to close the door. Whew! Just in time!

But that didn't stop Joshua from saying, "You're late, Smella."

Uh oh. He was back.

"So," Lucy said, turning around in her chair to face him. "You've been out all week, Joshua . . . Joshua . . ." I could tell she was trying to think of something that rhymes with Joshua, but nothing does. "Throw-up boy," she said.

That's the nicest thing about Lucy. When you're friends with her, she sticks up for you.

"That's enough," Mrs. Finkel said. "No Calling Out is a Ground Rule, and so is No Name-Calling."

"It's not on the list," Joshua said, calling out again.

"I'm adding it today," Mrs. Finkel said. "And it's going to be strictly enforced. Now, let's get started."

She made morning announcements, which included that Lucy and I would be the first pair presenting our current events reports right after snack. Of course she didn't say the secret part of our presentation—that we had newspapers to hand out, too.

With everything that had happened to Penny that morning, I'd forgotten that I was really nervous. But now I remembered. All through math and spelling, I had the jumpy nervous feeling, kind of like Pop Rocks were exploding in my stomach. It was hard to pay attention. During our quiet reading period, I tried to concentrate on the words in my book, but in my head I kept thinking about what I was going to say out loud, and how everyone would be looking at me.

Then Mrs. Finkel clapped her hands, and it was snack time. Lucy rushed over to my desk. "Do you have the envelope?" she asked.

"Yup."

"Good," she said. "Where is it?"

"In my backpack."

"You should keep it there so no one sees," she said. "You know it's still PB for a few more minutes, even from each other."

She was talking in code, even though

none of our other friends had come over to us.

I shook my head. "I know what you wrote about."

"What?! You read it! But you pinky-sweared you wouldn't."

"I didn't read it," I said. "I don't break pinky swears. It was just that Penny thought PB stood for Penny Batts, and she opened the envelope and told me what she saw."

"You should have plugged up your ears so you couldn't hear her."

"It all happened so fast, and she was really sad," I said.

A few feet away I heard people laughing and I glanced over at Talisa, Arielle, and Evie. "That was your best one!" Evie said. I bet Talisa had just told a knock-knock joke. I wished I were there with them to hear it.

The end of our PB couldn't come fast enough.

"I was thinking," Lucy said, "when we do our presentation, I should go first, because my last name comes first."

Mrs. Finkel clapped her hands, which meant the talking part of snack time was over.

A few minutes later, I was standing in front of the classroom, next to Lucy. Twenty-one sets of eyes were staring back at us: the other twenty kids in my class, plus Mrs. Finkel.

"So," Lucy began. "I'm going to tell you a little bit about the current event that I first found out about last Sunday, and it's STILL happening. I think it's important, and it affected my life, too, because of traffic. But let me explain. I was at Stella's house, and we were reading the newspaper with her dad. Which is a funny coincidence when you think about it. We were reading the paper, and the next day Mrs. Finkel gave us the assignment to read the paper. But anyway, as I was saying . . ."

Lucy went on to talk about what happened that day—how we found Penny Jr., and held a fish funeral, and then went to Man's Best Friend to find the fish who looked most like Penny Jr., and how on the way home got stuck in traffic around the Somers Playhouse, which is being turned into the Esther Smyth Arts Center. That way everyone would remember the woman who founded it—people in her family, and people who never even knew her, like us.

The whole time she was talking, I was thinking about something. Can you guess what it was? If you said it was that we should name something after Penny Jr., then you are right! Our whole family would remember her—especially Penny, and anyone else who came over would know all about Penny Jr., even if they never got to meet her.

"If you drive on Camden Road, you'll see the building too, and maybe you'll even get stuck in traffic," Lucy said. "In conclusion, I think it's a nice idea to name things after people so you always remember them. But I don't like traffic very much, so I hope they finish fixing up the building soon. That's it. The end."

Kids clapped, and Mrs. Finkel said, "Thank you, Lucy. That was a nice example of how the news affects our daily lives. All right, Stella. You're on."

All of a sudden my mouth felt dry, like I'd eaten a whole lot of chocolate fudge but didn't have any milk to drink. And my hands felt sticky, like I was working the cotton-candy machine and didn't wash my hands. The Pop Rocks were back in my stomach. Actually they were poppier than Pop Rocks. If Pop Rocks could do jumping jacks, that was what was in my stomach!

Uh oh. When I told Arielle I'd switch weeks with her, I didn't think it would feel like this. But now I wished I was back to being week seven, even if it meant being with

Joshua, because then I wouldn't have to be up here right now, with everyone watching me.

But wait. Mrs. Finkel had given Arielle some advice for when everyone is watching. You focus on just one person, and then it's not like you're giving a big presentation to your whole class. It's like you're just having a regular conversation.

"Stella?" Mrs. Finkel said again. "You ready to go?"

I stared at Evie.

Please, look back at me. Even if you're mad. Just look back at me. So I can pretend I'm talking right to you.

I clicked my heels together three times, so gently that no one could see. But right then, at the last click, Evie turned and looked at me.

"Yes, I'm ready," I said. "I'm going to talk about something that's going to be in the paper TODAY. And that is big news at our store, Batts Confections. There's a big change at Batts Confections, and it affects me because I'm Stella Batts, and it affects the rest of the people in this class, because everyone here loves our store—now you're going to love it even more!"

I wasn't nervous anymore, even though everyone was looking at me, because it wasn't so bad, once I started talking. Everyone was watching me, but in a good way, like they cared about what I was saying. I went on to tell them all the things in the candy arcade, and how I hoped they would all come to see it.

"Yeah!" Joshua said.

"Joshua!" Mrs. Finkel said.

"That's okay," I said. "That's the end. I'm done with my presentation."

Kids started clapping again, and I got that hot feeling you get in your cheeks when you start to blush. I knew my face was getting redder. But not super red like Red Hots candies. More like the pinky red of a piece of bubble gum.

The clapping stopped and Lucy said, "Now we have something to hand out."

But before we could, Mrs. Finkel said, "Stella, I'd hoped you'd read the paper this week, not just report on something in your own store."

"But I did read the paper," I told her. "I read about the building on Camden, like Lucy did. And I read about our mayor, and I read about the heat wave."

Wow, Dad was right. There was A LOT of information in the newspaper!

"I just decided to report on the thing that affected me most," I said. "Isn't that what I was supposed to do?"

I felt nervous all over again. The Pop Rocks were back in my stomach.

But Mrs. Finkel smiled. "Yes, that's exactly what you were supposed to do. Maybe I'll take Evan to Batts Confections this weekend. You can sit down now. You too, Lucy."

"But wait!" Joshua called out.

"Joshua, you know that No Calling Out is a Ground Rule," Mrs. Finkel said.

"But . . ." Joshua sputtered. "But they said

they had things to hand out."

"He's right," I said. "We do."

"Oh yes," Mrs. Finkel said. "Pass out the papers, girls."

"Mrs. Finkel?" I asked. "Is it okay if just Lucy passes them out? Because there's something I really need to do."

CHAPTER 10

Stella Jr.

I told Mrs. Finkel about how sad Penny had been that morning, and what my idea was, and how I really needed to speak to her as soon as possible. "Snack is over, but you can speak to her after school," she said.

"Can't I speak to her now?" I asked. "Please. It's so important. She's going to be sad all day."

I could tell she was going to say no, and my eyes started to feel watery, like I'd just eaten spicy Red Hots candies. It's sad when someone is sad and you know how to make them feel better and you're not allowed to do it until later.

"How about a compromise?" Mrs. Finkel said. "We have a couple more lessons before lunchtime. I'll let you head over to the kindergarten room then, and you can be a few minutes late to the cafeteria, okay?"

"Okay," I said. "Thanks."

When the lunch bell rang, Mrs. Finkel told everyone to line up—everyone except for me. "Stella, you may go now, but you need to bring a buddy."

"Where's she going?" Joshua asked, and before Mrs. Finkel could even answer, he started to yell. "Pick me! Pick me! Pick me!"

"She won't be picking anyone who doesn't obey the Ground Rules," Mrs. Finkel said.

I wouldn't pick Joshua, even if he did. "Can I pick Evie?" I asked.

"Yes," Mrs. Finkel said. "Go on, you two. You have ten minutes."

I didn't know if Evie even wanted to be my buddy, but now she sort of had to be. We walked out into the hall and I told her we were going to Penny's class. "She didn't know about her fish until she read Lucy's article this morning," I said. "She's really upset. But I have an idea that might make her feel an eensy weensy bit better."

"I know how she feels," Evie told me. "You can be quite upset when your pet dies."

"Yeah, you can," I said.

"And you can be quite upset when people

don't tell you things."

"I'm sorry, Evie," I said. "If it makes you feel any better, I think you can be quite upset when your best friend in Somers is mad at you, and you know it's all your fault."

"It makes me feel a little bit better," Evie said.

"Will you stop being mad if I promise no more secrets?"

"Do you promise?" Evie asked.

"I promise," I said. "No more secrets. . . . Except . . ."

"Except what?"

"Well sometimes you have to keep secrets. Like the secret recipe for fudge at Batts Confections, or a secret surprise party."

"Is there a secret surprise party?" she asked.

I shook my head. "Nope. But what if there

was one? Would I have to tell you?"

"I guess not," she said.

"Okay," I said. "No more secrets that aren't good ones like that. I pinky swear."

"Pinky swear," she said.

We hooked pinkies. "Hey, do you want to come with me to the store after school? I can show you the arcade."

"That would be lovely!"

We got to Penny's classroom. The door was open and all the kids were sitting in a big circle on the floor, spelling words out in a song. I forgot you do things like that in kindergarten—sit on the floor and sing things. By the time you are in first grade, you have a desk and you have to talk in a regular voice.

I spotted Penny and Zoey on the far side of the room. The teacher, Mrs. Griffin, was

sitting on Penny's other side. Penny saw me too, but she didn't smile or wave. Instead she turned her head away from me. I clicked my heels together and made a wish for Penny to look up at me, but it didn't work.

"Hang on, kids," Mrs. Griffin said. "We have a couple visitors." She stood up and walked over to us. "Why, Stella Batts, I haven't seen you in this room for a while. Can I help you with anything?"

I glanced over at Penny, who was still not looking at me. "I was just worried about my sister," I said.

"Penny? Can you come here a minute, please?"

Penny stood up and walked over to us. But she still wouldn't look at me.

"Penny, I'm really sorry I didn't tell you about the fish," I said. "But I have an idea to make you feel a little better."

"Girls, I'm going to head back to the group," Mrs. Griffin said. "Why don't you step into the hall and talk, okay?"

Penny came with Evie and me. "We don't have much time," Evie said. "Mrs. Finkel said ten minutes and it's already been—" she paused to glance at her watch. Yes, Evie wears a watch like a grown-up. "Six!"

"I'm only talking to you to tell you that I'm not talking to you," Penny said.

"Okay, you don't have to talk anymore," I told her. "Just listen. I know you're really sad about Penny Jr., but maybe part of the reason why you're so sad is because you didn't get to come to the funeral, and now you don't have anything to remember her by. You didn't read the rest of Lucy's article, but it was all about naming the big Somers Playhouse after an old lady who died, so everyone would remember her. I thought that would be a nice thing to do for Penny Jr., and then every time we passed the Penny Jr. place, we'd think about her."

"We can't name the Playhouse after Penny Jr.," Penny said. "It wouldn't be fair to the old lady. Besides, I don't think we're allowed to change the names of buildings. We're just kids."

"You're right," I said. "But we can name something in our own house after her. Something that would be perfect for a little goldfish."

"Like where?"

"Like maybe the shelf in the kitchen where we keep the fish bowls. We could call it the Penny Jr. Shelf, and we could make a big sign, and even draw a picture of her. What do you think?"

"I'm not such a good drawer," Penny said.

"I am," Evie told her. "I can help you."

"Great, Evie can help," I said. "Then Fudge and the new Penny Jr. will swim on the Penny Jr. Shelf, and we'll always remember her."

"All right," Penny said. "Let's do that."

Evie looked at her watch. "We really must get going," she said.

We hugged Penny good-bye and she

pulled open the classroom door. But just before she disappeared onto the other side, she poked her head back out. "Wait, I have one more thing to tell you. Penny Jr. was special. She was one of a kind."

"I know," I said.

"So I'm going to give my new fish a different name. Can you guess what it is?"

"We don't have time to guess," I reminded her.

"All right, I'll tell you," Penny said. "Stella Jr.!"

Sneak preview of

Stella Batts

Superstar

Book

Discovered

"Stella Stella bo bella banana fana fo fella me my mo mella . . . STELLA!"

Stella is my name, and the person singing was my sister, Penny. She was sitting across from me at a booth in Brody's Grill, the restaurant Mom and Dad had taken us to for dinner. It was a Monday, and we usually eat at home during the week. But that day, nobody felt like cooking, and besides Brody's Grill is our favorite restaurant.

"Ba ba ba ba ba ba ba," said my brother, Marco, singing nonsense.

"Penny." Now that was Mom. "Keep it down, please."

"It's Opposite Day!" Penny cried. "That means you want me to keep it up!"

"Penelope Jane," Mom said. "Inside voice. Now."

"Sometimes Mrs. Finkel tells Joshua to use an inside voice," I said. "That's a Ground Rule in our class, you know."

"It's a Ground Rule at this restaurant, too," Mom said. "So all of the customers can enjoy their meals. All right, Pen?"

"Pa pa pa pa pa pa pa," Marco said.

"I think Marco's saying your name, Penny," Dad said.

"Use your inside voice, Marco!" Penny told him.

"Shhh, Penny," Mom said. "He's just a baby. He doesn't know any better. But you're five, and you do."

Penny folded her arms across her chest. I wondered if she was going to start wishing she were a baby again, too. That happened when Marco was first born. Penny was jealous she didn't get to be youngest anymore.

The waitress came over to our table. "Can I bring you anything? Coffee, tea?" she asked.

"Just the check whenever you get a chance," Dad said.

"*I'm a little teapot,*" Penny began to sing.

"Penny," Mom said in a warning voice.

"What? I'm using my inside voice—my inside singing voice." And she started again. "*I'm a little teapot, shortened spout. Here is my handle, here is my spout. When I get all steamed up hear me shout. Tip me over and pour me out!"*

"Penelope Jane, that's enough," Mom said.

"Those weren't even the right words," I said.

"They were so," she said.

"They were not. It goes like this." I started to sing, *"I'm a little teapot—"*

"Stella, not you too," Mom said.

"I just need to teach her the right words," I said. "I'll be so quick. *I'm a little teapot, SHORT and STOUT. Here is my handle, here is my spout."*

"All right," Mom said. "We've got it."

"Excuse me," a man said. "I'm sorry to interrupt. I couldn't help but hear the concert going on at your table."

"I'm so sorry we were bothering you," Mom told him. "See, girls, this man who was sitting clear across the restaurant could hear you singing. Now what do you say?"

"Sorry," I mumbled.

"Sorry," Penny said too.

"Oh, no need to be sorry," the man said. "I rather enjoyed what I was hearing. I wondered, do you do it professionally?"

"Like as a job?" I asked.

"Exactly," the man said. "I'm a casting director with Auditions Unlimited."

"What's a casting director?" Penny asked.

"Someone who decides what people get to be in movies and TV and stuff like that," I told her.

"Movies and TV?" Penny asked. "Really?"

"Really," the man said. "Here, let me give your parents a card."

He handed it to Dad.

"I want to see," Penny said.

"Me too," I said. "I'll read it to you." I took

it and read out loud:

Hal Lewis, Director
Auditions Unlimited
101 Sanderson Drive
Somers, California

"All right, Stel," Mom said. "I'll take that now." I handed the business card to Mom.

"Are we going to be famous?" Penny asked.

"I think we're getting a little ahead of ourselves here," Dad told her.

"Right now I'm looking for a young girl for a little scene in a TV show I'm casting. And I think your daughter—your older daughter—might just be perfect for it."

His older daughter. That was me! I was the oldest kid in our family. "Me?" I asked.

"Really?"

"Yes, really," Hal said.

Oh my goodness! Oh my goodness! Oh my goodness!

Courtney Sheinmel

Courtney Sheinmel is the author of several books for middle-grade readers, including *Sincerely* and *All the Things You Are*. Like Stella Batts, she was born in California and has a younger sister, but unlike Stella, her parents never owned a candy store. Courtney now lives in New York City. Visit her online at www.courtneysheinmel. com where you can find out more about all the Stella Batts books.

Jennifer A. Bell

Jennifer A. Bell is an illustrator whose work can be found on greeting cards, in magazines, and in more than a dozen children's books. She lives in Minneapolis, Minnesota, with her husband and son. Visit her online at www.JenniferABell.com.

Meet Stella and friends online
at www.stellabatts.com

Praise for Stella Batts

"Sheinmel has a great ear for the dialogue and concerns of eight-year-old girls. Bell's artwork is breezy and light, reflecting the overall tone of the book. This would be a good choice for fans of Barbara Park's 'Junie B. Jones' books."

— *School Library Journal*

"First in a series featuring eight-year-old Stella, Sheinmel's unassuming story, cheerily illustrated by Bell, is a reliable read for those first encountering chapter books. With a light touch, Sheinmel persuasively conveys elementary school dynamics; readers may recognize some of their own inflated reactions to small mortifications in likeable Stella, while descriptions of unique candy confections are mouth-watering."

— *Publishers Weekly*

"Why five stars? Because any book that can make a reader out of a child deserves five stars in my book! It's all about getting kids 'hooked' on reading."

— Pam Kramer, Examiner.com

"My daughter is nine years old and struggled with reading since Kindergarten. Recently we found the Stella Batts books and she has fallen in love with them. She has proudly read them all and she can't wait till #6. We can't thank you enough. Her confidence with reading has improved 100%. It brings tears to my eyes to see her excited about reading. Thanks."

— K.M. Anchorage, Alaska